The Story of C

& Her Flags - From 1849 to the Present

Continued from *The Story of Early California & her flags to color*

HARRY KNILL, drawings by ALAN ARCHAMBAULT

We'll teach them where the Bear flag flies
There's no surrender nor surprise—
There ev'ry soldier wins or dies.

With Freedom's banner is unroll'd
The standard from the land of gold . . .
Strange was the flag, still stranger seem'd

The small white hand in which it gleam'd:
And much they marveled, one so fair
And young, their battle-flag should bear . . .

—*J. Henry Rogers*, 1865

Mrs. Reed, on the cover and here, went east to the Civil War with her husband Capt. J. Sewell Reed, who led the California Hundred (see inside). Mrs. Reed was a sometime standard bearer, according to epic poet Rogers. On February 23, 1863, at Drainsville, Virginia, while fighting the wiley Confederate Mosby, Capt. Reed and thirteen men were killed. Mrs. Reed is shown at the war's end with the heroic unit's sacred banner, with the actions inscribed on it and as it is seen today in the Capitol, Sacramento. There is no relic more sacred in our State's historical treasury than this banner. Many Californians died around it fighting to end injustice.

THE HOUNDS, 1849

"They took this name from going throughout the place every night at eleven o'clock and barking like hounds." Letter, July, '49

SAN FRANCISCO SOCIETY OF REGULATORS

Soulé, *Annals of San Francisco*, 1855
Letter to Nantucket, July 19, 1849,
Cal. Hist. Soc. Quarterly, v. 29

The Hounds:
"San Francisco was afflicted with a parcel of the veriest rogues and ruffians that ever haunted a community. The first intelligence of the discovery of gold in California naturally sent thither the most daring and clever adventurers of blemished reputation. A little later came stray vagabonds from Australia, the choice of the convicted felons of Great Britain. The regiment of New York volunteers had been disbanded, and many of the most noted blackguards of the country turned out to have been formerly in that corps."

THE CHILEAN WAR NEAR MOKELUMNE HILL, 1849

Thousands of Chileans arrived early in the Gold Rush, for they were already on the Pacific coast when the glad tidings got out. They found the best claims, and many were skilled miners. Gringos arriving later grew jealous, and Gen. Smith futilely ordered all foreigners out of the mines. Then the Hounds viciously attacked the Chilean district at the bottom of Telegraph Hill in San Francisco. A little later, a huge foreign miners' tax outraged the Chileans.

The "Chileño, who when their blood is up are very devils."
—Perkins, Sonora '49

Flag: white and red stripes; blue canton with a white star.

V. Pérez Rosales, *Cal. Adventure*, 1947
J. J. Ayers, *Gold and Sunshine*, 1922
El Comercio de Valparaiso, Aug. 17, 1949

In December '49, miners of Iowa Hill ordered Dr. Concha and his company at Chile Gulch to leave their rich diggings. The doctor armed his 60 men and marched on the Iowa Hillmen; two were killed and 16 captured—and escaped and then captured the Chileans. On the Tuolumne River, A Chilean flag was raised in defiance of the American "skunks."

THE GREAT REPUBLIC OF ROUGH AND READY

THE REPUBLIC OF ROUGH AND READY
April 7, 1850

Rough and Ready was a mining town on the Yuba River, "located" in 1849 by the Rough and Ready Company from Wisconsin, ten men led by Captain A.A. Townsend, who had served with General Zachary "Old Rough and Ready" Taylor. It was known to have the most beautifully colored gold in the region, and thousands of miners soon went there. A government of three was appointed to rule the place, and so successful were they that Colonel Brundage came up with the idea of forming a separate and independent sovereignty, to be called the "State of Rough and Ready." On April 7, 1850, it was constituted and Brundage was elected president. This affair lasted until the Fourth of July, when the sight of the glorious Stars and Stripes and the potations surrounding them brought the Rough and Readymen back to the fold.

There were a good many black '49ers; some, who came by way of Mexico, were received "with far more distinction" than anyone else. And in the gold mines, "there prevailed at that time a singular superstition in regard to black. . . men . . . it was a common belief that they had luck in seeking for gold," wrote Major Downie. He and Albert Callis who "I believe, was a runaway slave," took out 17 oz. of gold on Monday, 24 on Tuesday, 29 on Wednesday, and early on Thursday, 40 oz., or $55,000 at current prices (since it was tax free, you might double that); see G.W. Evans, *Mexican Gold Trail*, ed. G. Dumke, 1945, and W.Downie, *Hunting for Gold*, 1893

California and Oregon are too distant to be members of the Union. It would be better for them to be an independent government.

Old Rough and Ready,
Polk's Diary, March 4, 1849

Hittell, 3, 280
Shinn, Mining Camps, 225

Flag: blue field, white letters on field, white scroll with red letters, from the present flag, date unknown.

THE CONSTITUTIONAL CONVENTION, MONTEREY, 1849

The Rev. Mr. Colton, U.S.N., *alcalde* of Monterey 1846-8, set his jailed malefactors abuilding a magnificent schoolhouse, dubbed "Colton Hall." It was here that the governor, Brig. General Bennett Riley, had a convention of forty-eight men meet on August 1, 1849, to frame a state constitution or a territorial government. Statehood was adopted. A declaration of rights was made: there would be no slavery in California. Boundaries had to be determined; should California include the new Mormon colony far to the east? A Great Seal was designed; all the districts wanted something in it: a miner, the Bay, the Bear, grapes, a ship. When, finally, the constitution was finished and signed, Old Glory was run up and the framers went to see Governor Riley. Captain Sutter presented the document to the old soldier. There were many cheers and tears.

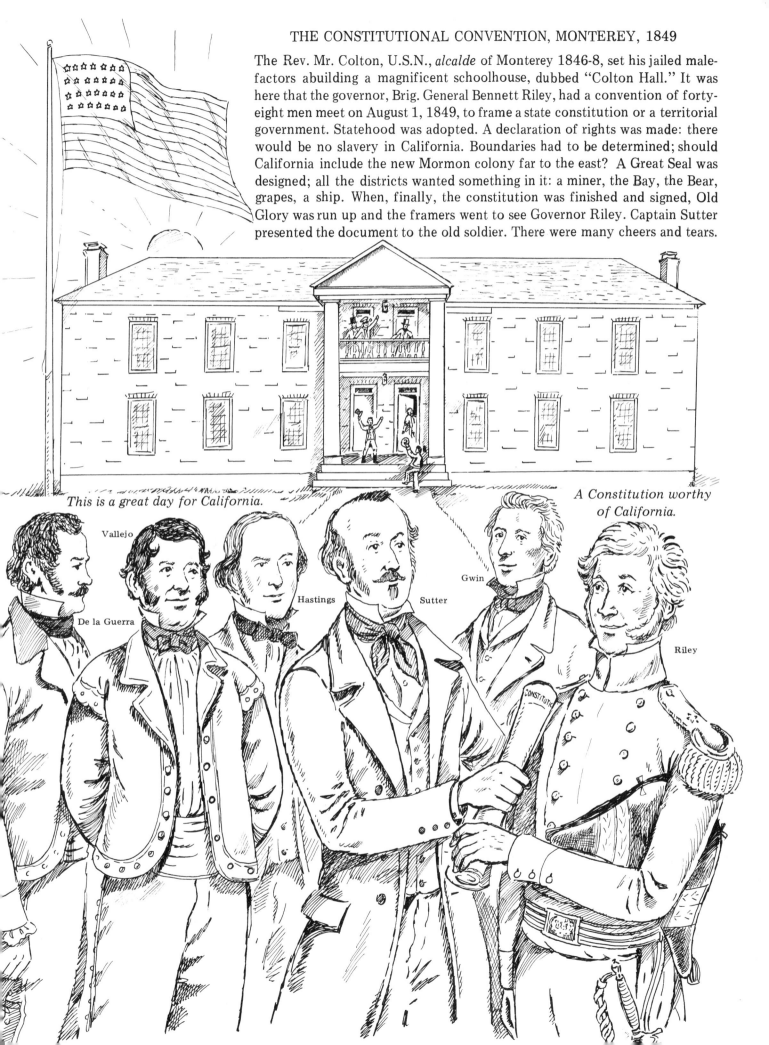

This is a great day for California.

A Constitution worthy of California.

Vallejo

De la Guerra

Hastings

Sutter

Gwin

Riley

CALIFORNIA AND TEXAS
Colonel Jack Hays, Hero of
The Texas Rangers, Sheriff
of San Francisco, 1850

*A Ranger is no better
than his horse.*

THE TEXAS RANGERS

1st TEXAS VOLS

HAYS
FOR
SHERIFF
SAN FRANCISCO

Texas flags: blue fields, white
stars, red and white stripes

Flag: S. Reid, Jr., *McCulloch's Texas
Rangers,* 1847, p. 174. See too, Soule,
Annals of San Francisco, 1855, 270-2.

Before 1846, Californians of every political persuasion had long wanted to emulate Texas: break away from Mexico's nominal rule, form a new, independent country, and then join the U.S., Britain or France. In the 1846 war, the Texas Rangers played many memorable parts, and after the war roving Texans in droves came to golden California. And the foremost was the celebrated Texas Ranger, young Col. Jack Hays, who ran for Sheriff of San Francisco in 1850. He ran against rich Col. Bryant, who was determined to spare no expense to win the election. Bryant's hotel was covered with beautiful flags and banners of every form; he had a band of music playing and free lunches for all. On March 29, 1850, Col. Hays' friends formed a parade, with their own band of music, and soon all the plaza was covered with banners and flags. During the election the next day, it was early evident that Col. Hays was the people's favorite, whereupon Bryant's party made another grand display on the plaza. Then Col. Hays, mounted upon a fiery black charger, suddenly appeared, exhibiting some of the finest specimens of horsemanship ever witnessed. The sight of the hero settled the question. The vast majority of the votes went to the "Texan Ranger."

President Polk said in 1848 that if California was left without a government for another year, "it might be lost to the Union . . . they would probably organize an independent government, calling it the California or Pacific Republic." Military rule lingered, for Congress had not given California a government because of the slavery issue. So Californians decided to organize a provincial government. A convention met in Monterey in September, 1849, and a constitution stating that slavery would never be tolerated was signed on October 14. The "best legis-lature California ever had" followed; Gwin and Frémont were chosen as Senators to go to Washington, where they urged that California be admitted immediately to the Union. They were opposed by Calhoun: two new senators from a free state bothered southerners. He predicted civil war. Still, the Senate passed a bill for admission and the House passed it, too. It was approved on September 9. On October 18, a beflagged steamer, the *Oregon*, sailed through the Golden Gate with a banner which said CALIFORNIA IS A STATE. Guns boomed, and the flag, with another star of paper pinned on was run up on the lofty staff. . ."

The Grand Celebration
October 29, 1850
OF CALIFORNIA'S ADMISSION
TO THE UNION,
September 9, 1850

Sources:
lithographs by C. Pollard, F. Marryatt and S.F. newspapers, etc.

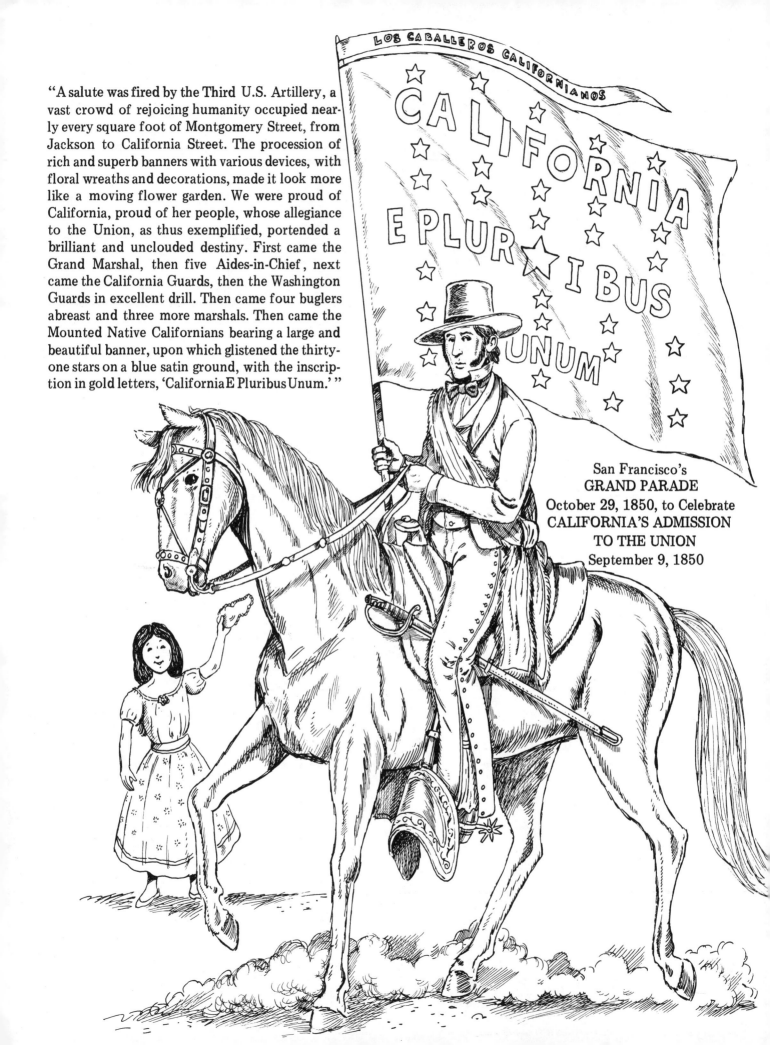

"A salute was fired by the Third U.S. Artillery, a vast crowd of rejoicing humanity occupied nearly every square foot of Montgomery Street, from Jackson to California Street. The procession of rich and superb banners with various devices, with floral wreaths and decorations, made it look more like a moving flower garden. We were proud of California, proud of her people, whose allegiance to the Union, as thus exemplified, portended a brilliant and unclouded destiny. First came the Grand Marshal, then five Aides-in-Chief, next came the California Guards, then the Washington Guards in excellent drill. Then came four buglers abreast and three more marshals. Then came the Mounted Native Californians bearing a large and beautiful banner, upon which glistened the thirty-one stars on a blue satin ground, with the inscription in gold letters, 'California E Pluribus Unum.'"

LOS CABALLEROS CALIFORNIANOS

CALIFORNIA
E PLURIBUS UNUM

San Francisco's
GRAND PARADE
October 29, 1850, to Celebrate
CALIFORNIA'S ADMISSION
TO THE UNION
September 9, 1850

Then came the Society of California Pioneers, with this beautiful banner painted with the State Seal with Minerva, goddess of industry and good government, in the center, presiding over the building of the state. She encourages the arts and protects the home. Keep at it, old girl. Then came the officers of the Army and Navy followed by officers and soldiers of the Frémont Battalion and First Regiment of New York Volunteers. Next were the Orators of the Day, Clergymen, consuls and representatives of foreign governments, and Queen Victoria's subjects.

In a Chinese hotel in San Francisco a little later, "the proprietor took us into his private room, and showed us a flag he had received from home; it was twenty feet long and twelve broad of the nicest crape, crimson, the design an immense dragon, wrought with gold thread, the same on both sides. . . with enormous eyes gazing at the moon, and some Chinese figures, making the most magnificent thing of the kind I ever saw, but there is no place in the world but this where there is wind enough to float such an extensive affair."
—Letter of Mary Megguier, May 30, 1852, Huntington Library

"The Chinese appeared in their rich native costume, presenting a fine appearance, with an elegant blue banner.* The triumphal car came next, with thirty boys representing the thirty states, each with the national arms with the name of a state. Then in the center of this magnificent car appeared a smiling little girl, dressed in white with gold and silver gauze floating gracefully from her head. She held a shield upon which was inscribed: 'California—the Union, it must and shall be preserved.' Then came the mayor, recorder, aldermen and judicial officers of the city, with a large banner inscribed: 'San Francisco—The Commercial Emporium of the Pacific.' Next came the police department, with an elegant blue satin banner surmounted with a golden eagle, inscribed 'San Francisco Police Department—Semper Paratus.' "

* "In 1850 at the celebration in San Francisco of the admission of California into the Union, the Chinese were given the post of honor. . . and placed directly after the state and city officials in the long line," wrote farmer Stuart of Sonoma twenty-seven years later. "It was their labor that made California what it was. It was their men . . . that had mainly built the railroads, cleared the farms, reclaimed a million acres of swamp and overflowed land, planted the orchards and vineyards, reaped the crops and gathered the fruits, dug and sacked the potatoes, manufactured the woolen and other goods, cleaned up the tailings of the hydraulic mines, scraped the bed-rock of the exhausted placers, built the cities. . . Nearly everything of value had been done by them."-Hittell, *History of California*, v.4, 622-3

After a lithograph of Cooke & Le Count, 1852

The Fireman's Journal and Military Gazette, July 12, 1856, etc.

"THE FIRE DEPARTMENT is always one of the chief features in public processions."

Annals of San Francisco

Then came the Howard Engine Company Number Three (old Boston firemen in blue shirts and black caps) with their engine tastefully decorated with flags and rosettes. Then came the California Company Number Four with engine equally decorated. Then came the Monumental Fire Company Number Six (of old Baltimore firemen). Their axmen wore black pants and caps and pink silk shirts.

SAN FRANCISCO

KNICKERBOCKER ENGINE CO.

NUMBER FIVE

Then came the Saint Francis Hook and Ladder Company, with a richly trimmed blue satin banner inscribed "We destroy to save." In the years 1850, '51 and '52, the principal work at fires fell to the hook and ladder companies because it was impossible to obtain water for the engines . . .

Soon after came the Knickerbocker Engine Company Number Five—red shirts and black caps. The San Francisco fire department was set in motion on Christmas, 1849, the day after the first great fire. David C. Broderick and other old New York firemen were among the founders. Their fire companies had been used to disputing by fist fights the honor of putting out fires. Broderick became foreman of the Empire Engine Company Number One, also a fighting political organization. He soon after became U.S. Senator from California, a fierce anti-slavery Democrat when President Buchanan's Democracy was pro-slavery, and when southerners controlled California. He was killed in a duel for this; then did California sentiment switch towards getting rid of that vile institution and staying with the Union.

The Knickerbocker Banner was presented by John Hoxie, amidst "the genial old Dutch hospitality." *The Fireman's Journal and Military Gazette,* October 16, 1856

The Dutch flag of Old New Amsterdam: top stripe orange red, middle white, bottom blue

Next came the Sansome Hook and Ladder Company Number Three, wearing red shirts and black pants and caps. They were always in charge of the powder magazine for blowing up buildings at fires. Their carriage was decked in magnificent style, with five banners as shown here. Over the carriage was formed a pyramid of short ladders, decked with flowers, upon which perched a live American eagle. The pyramid seemed to form an appropriate arbor for "The Belle of the

Pacific," a most beautiful little lass of some eight or ten years of age, said to have been the first child born of American parents in California. The air resounded with huzzas whenever "the Belle" made her appearance.

SANSOME HOOK and LADDER COMPANY NO. 3

ORGANIZED JUNE 14, 1850

WE RAZE TO SAVE

A TREASU FOUND

This flag scene a little later: "A splendid silk flag will be presented to the Lafayettes by a lady." *Fireman's and Military Gazette,* May 31, 1856

The French flag: blue, white, red, gold letters; gilt helmet, blue uniform, red collar front, gilt No. 2

LAFAYETTE
HOOK and LADDER
CIE. NO.
2
SAN FRANCISCO
CALIFORNIE

Next came the boatmen with a decorated boat, with banners inscribed "United we pull a more effective Stroke," "By Commerce we Thrive," "In Union we pull Together." Then came a car of the Pacific Topographical Society upon which was the first printing press made in California, printing for the crowds Mrs. Wills's Ode:

> Rejoice! Hear ye not o'er the hills of the East
> The sound of our welcome to Liberty's Union?
> Pledge high! for we join in the mystical feast
> That our forefathers hallowed at Freedom's communion!
>
> . . .
>
> And the Band of the Union, oh, long may it be
> The hope of th'oppressed and the shield of the free!

It was sung to the tune of the 'Star Spangled Banner.' Many more followed in the parade, and afterwards there were ceremonies at the plaza. All the bands together played 'Hail Columbia' and then the 'Marseillaise,' for there were many Frenchmen in California, and it was the French who had helped our country of liberty at its birth. Afterwards cannon boomed again, small arms fired, firecrackers banged, and fireworks lit up the evening. It was a glorious day to celebrate an event for which we too are happy.

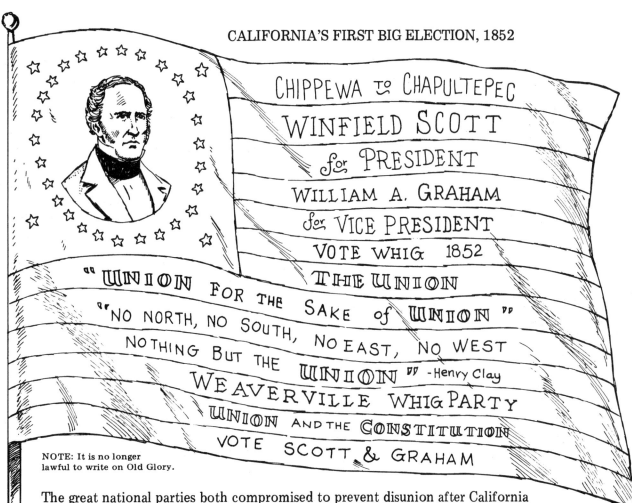

CHIPPEWA to CHAPULTEPEC
WINFIELD SCOTT
for PRESIDENT
WILLIAM A. GRAHAM
for VICE PRESIDENT
VOTE WHIG 1852
THE UNION
"UNION FOR THE SAKE of UNION"
"NO NORTH, NO SOUTH, NO EAST, NO WEST
NOTHING BUT THE UNION" -Henry Clay
WEAVERVILLE WHIG PARTY
UNION AND THE CONSTITUTION
VOTE SCOTT & GRAHAM

NOTE: It is no longer
lawful to write on Old Glory.

Note: Gen. Scott was known as "Old Fuss and Feathers" because of his military dress; Mr. Graham was from North Carolina, the "Tar State." Daniel Webster, when he heard of the nomination, labeled it "feathers and tar—tar and feathers," and so Scott was ridiculed and lost the election. Henry Clay and Webster were the great leaders of the Whig Party; both died in 1852, and after this election the party waned away.

The great national parties both compromised to prevent disunion after California was admitted as a free state. The northern Whigs tried to placate the south by nominating a non-political military man, General Scott, for President. The south accepted General Pierce, a northern Democrat, after the election. The Whigs' platform had been subsidies for ships and railroads, lands for farmers and miners. Four years later, the Knownothings, the secretive American Party who were against the foreign born, gathered up the old Whigs and defeated the Democrats. They were also apologists for slavery, so the Republican party was organized in Sacramento by citizens opposed to that vile institution. The few founders included C.P. Huntington, Mark Hopkins, Leland Stanford and the Crockers; their great orator was Colonel Edward Baker—"he rivalled Cicero himself." Buchanan was nominated by the Democrats, Fillmore by the Knownothings, and the Republican flag was Freedom, Frémont and the Railroad. They were opposed by the "Sea-serpent party (Fillmore's), in consideration of its having a fishy smell, being eely and oily and destitute of a backbone... There was only one great national question: whether the general government shall be longer under the control of the slave power. . . or whether it shall subserve the purposes for which our fathers designed it—as a nursery of freedom, and the asylum for the oppressed of all lands—and shall it afford no relief to the oppressed of our own?" The next campaign, 1860, the Democrats split between Douglas (northern) and Breckenridge (southern) and Lincoln was elected. Fort Sumter was fired on on April 12, 1861.

SCOTT FOREVER!

"We have erected a pole 130 feet high with a Scott and Graham flag, of the largest size."
—*Franklin A. Buck*, Weaverville, September 22, 1852

VOTE EARLY!

VOTE OFTEN HUZZAH!

To prevent the likes of the Hounds from again taking over and to help maintain order and security, a permanent volunteer military was established. The First California Guard was organized in 1849, of picked young men, veterans of the recent war, full of esprit de corps. In 1850 the Washington Guards were established, and the next year, the Empire Guards of that fire company. Indian disturbances that year added the San Francisco Rangers, the Aldridge Rangers, the Marion Rifle Corps, the Eureka Light Horse Guards, the National Lancers, and the San Francisco Blues. The Sutter Rifles of Sacramento joined the San Francisco companies on July 4, 1853, for a grand review by the venerable and immortal John A. Sutter, who had presented his Rifles with the flag shown.

Everyone knows about John A. Sutter (see our *Rosie & the Bear Flag*, for instance); in the early days he liked to be called the 'Commander of the Fortress of New Helvetia.' The title was none too good for him. A man who fed the hungry, clothed the naked, and comforted the sick. If it's true that Frémont brought the flood of people, old Sutter was there to welcome them."
—*T. Fallon*, Jan. 1, 1881

SUTTER RIFLES

ORGANIZED 26TH JUNE, 1852

THE CALIFORNIA MILITARY COMPANIES

General Sutter's uniform: blue, gold decoration; Captain Fry's uniform: green, red decoration; Flag: probably green, too, and red; See S.F. *Daily Herald*, October 30, 1850, S.F. *Alta*, May 24, 1852

"Our Fourth of July celebration, which came off at Rich Bar (Plumas County), was quite a respectable affair. I had the honor of making a flag for the occasion. The stripes were formed of cotton cloth and red calico, of which last gorgeous material, no possible place in Cal. is ever destitute. . . A large star in the center, covered with gold leaf, represented Cal. Humble as were the materials. . . this banner made quite a gay appearance, floating from the top of a lofty pine."

BETSY ROSS OF THE MINES
Mrs. Louise Knapp Smith Clappe (Dame Shirley)
July 4, 1852

And now the banner
of the free
Is in very deed our own
And 'mid the brother-
hood of States,
Not ours, the feeblest one.

Then proudly shout,
ye bushy men,
With throats all brown
and bare.
For lo! from 'midst
Our Flag's brave blue,
Leaps out a golden star.

The Poem of the Day

HUZZA
HUZZA

THE EMPIRE

THE FRENCH REVOLUTION

IN THE MINES

Murphys, Calaveras County, 1850

From staff:
blue-white-red

Allons
enfants!

There were revolutions in Europe in 1848, so thousands of Frenchmen joined the gold rush. The California legislature passed a law requiring all foreign miners to pay a monthly tax of $20 (1¼ oz. of gold, or $500 today). If they couldn't or wouldn't pay, they would have to leave. "I think we will have trouble between us soon. They are all well armed and live and travel in military style, having their officers, Music, Flags, &c.," wrote a miner. A letter with a false rumor of compatriots jailed in Sonora for refusing to pay reached the French camp at Murphys. Madame Louis, a tall, slim gambler, twenty-six years old, wearing a red shirt, dark pantaloons and an ostrich feather in a large sombrero, addressed the angry crowd: "My life for my countrymen. Let all who have a courageous heart follow our flag." She had a double-barrelled shotgun, two pistols and a big knife, as she led about 500 red-shirted French miners to "take Sonora by storm." On the way they met a Texan, who predicted that the excitement would all "end in a rat tail." And it did, when it was found that the tale of jailings was untrue.

*L. Fairchild, letter, Dec. 24, 1850
Scene: F. Gerstäcker, *Scènes de la Vie Californienne*, 1854

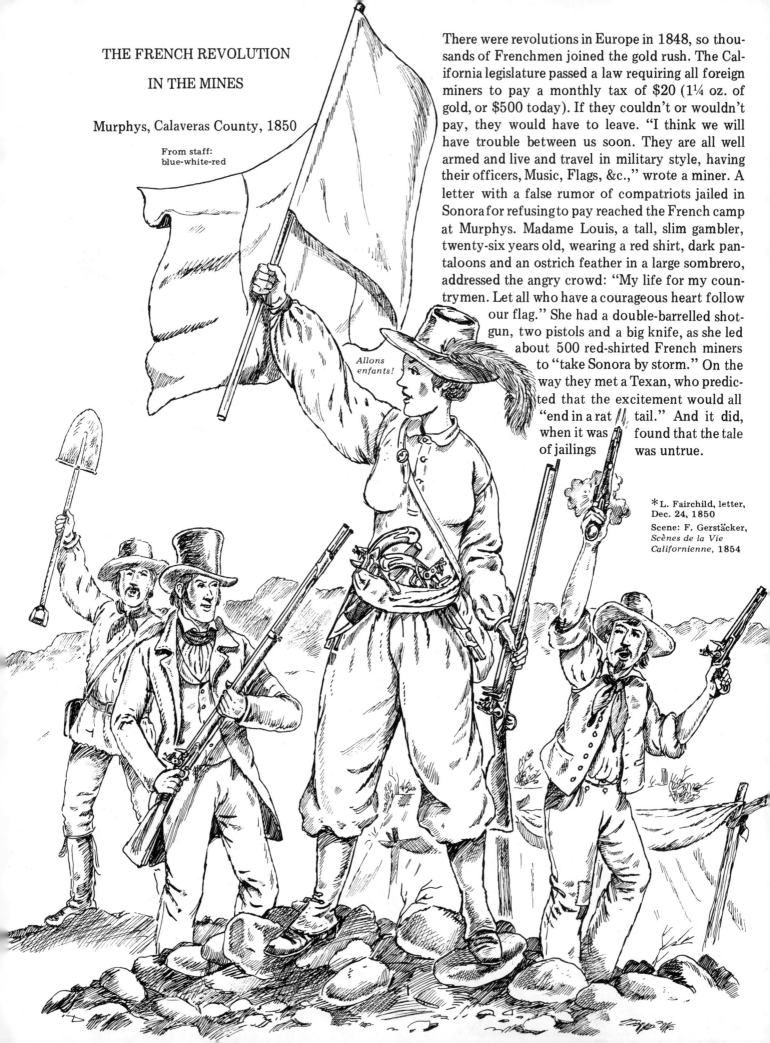

Mining became more difficult, and California was no longer amusing. The Marquis de Pindry, a noble French giant and bear hunter in Contra Costa County, recruited a band of compatriots to colonize the thought-to-be-rich mines of Old Sonora, Mexico. There he was mysteriously murdered. Then a gallant poet-adventurer, the tiny Count Raousset-Boulbon, recruited another army of Frenchmen who were tired of California for the next Sonoran adventure. He captured Hermosillo and soon tried to make Sonora his own independent state. He fell wildly in love with Antonia, the blond daughter of the chief of Altar, an enemy. But the conquest was lost at the Battle of Guaymas. His men were routed; among them were too many lawyers for harmony. The brave count was shot by firing squad on the beach, to the grief of the Sonoran ladies. His adventures had stirred up concern in Washington; the U.S. quickly made the Gadsden Purchase.

INDEPENDANCE DE LA SONORE!

Si, mille fois trompé,
tu conserves la foi,
Si tu luttes encore,
enfant! tu seras roi!

Count Gaston de
RAOUSSET-BOULBON
1853

See A. de Lachapelle,
Le Comte de Raous-
set-Boulbon, 1859,
p. 120

His coulors were
gold, black and red.
Red shirt.

WILLIAM WALKER THE FILIBUSTER, 1853

Restless Americans were so used to moving on to new territory that they just had to keep looking for more. What Austin had done in Texas, Frémont in California, others could do elsewhere. William Walker opened a recruiting office in San Francisco, announced he was sailing with an army from California to take Sonora. A strong defense awaited him there, so he sailed instead to capture La Paz. The Republic of Lower California was declared by President Walker, but the inhabitants rebelled. Then the capital was moved to bleak Todos Santos, where Walker's men drilled for the Sonoran invasion. The name was changed to the Republic of Sonora, divided into two states, Sonora and Lower California. He expected they would be annexed to the Union as slave states, since he was a southerner. The men didn't enjoy tramping in the desert, though, and many deserted. The few who remained were finally rescued from angry Mexican citizens by the U.S. Army. Walker later appeared in Nicaraugua with another filibuster army, misruled the country, was captured and shot.

Red-blue-red stripes, white stars, gray eyes, blue uniforms

See: Horace Bell, *Reminiscenses of a Ranger*, 1881; A. Woodward, *Repub. of Lower California*, 1966

Vice President Watson

THE INDOMITABLE LOLA MONTEZ

All great revolutions were owing to women.

In der Spanierin fand Liebe und Leben ich nur!

Flag: gold crown; white field, blue outer stripes; arms: center shield blue and white; upper right and lower left quarters, red and white; upper left, gold lion, lower right blue lion

Lola, short for Dolores, Montez, born in Ireland, raised in India, Scotland, England and France, was an actress, a dancer and an adventuress—and she conquered King Ludwig I of Bavaria in love. He made her Countess of Landsfeld. "Under her counsels," she wrote, "a total revolution afterwards took place." She supported popular rights and thus "became a fiend, a devil, a she-dragon" to displaced nobility. "The revolution broke out and drove her from power," so in 1852 she came to America and the next year she conquered San Francisco. There she did her Spider Dance, and roars rent the air. She married at Mission Dolores, went to Sacramento and there addressed a boisterous crowd: "You cowards, low blackguards, cringing dogs and lazy fellows!" Tremendous enthusiasm followed. She moved to Grass Valley with her parrot and poodle and found a pet grizzly bear. And there old European plotters talked of making Lola "Empress of California."

San Francisco in 1848 had 812 inhabitants; by the end of 1849 it had about 18,000. Social conduct there was deplorable: gambling and drinking, fights and brawls were everywhere. Thieves and rapscallions came to town in large numbers. Many of them were hardened old English convicts from the penal colonies in Australia who claimed that enough more were coming from there to take over. Late in '49 and in the '50s, San Francisco had a series of terrible fires which demolished the city; they were thought to have been purposely set. Justice was weak, so the famous Vigilance Committee was formed in 1851 to preserve lives and property. One Jenkins committed "a vile depredation" on June 10 and was directly hanged by the citizens. Then an old English villain, James Stuart, from Sydney, was caught. He confessed a myriad of crimes and was hung. Two more villains, Whittaker and MacKensie, met the same end. Evil-doers left town. In August, the Vigilance Committee,

with 700 members, suspended its operations. By 1855 there were about 75,000 people in San Francisco, and many were wild and bad. On November 18, General Richardson, the U.S. Marshal, was assassinated by Charles Cora, a fancy-dressing gambler, who was quickly arrested. Soon the old Vigilance Committee bell sounded. Cora, with eminent and able lawyers, was tried, but the jury reached no verdict. Then another crime took place on May 14, 1856: James Casey, editor of the *Sunday Times*, shot James King, editor of the *Evening Bulletin*. Members of the Vigilance Committee met and organized anew. Soon they numbered 2,600 men, organized into companies of 100. They were directed by Charles Doane from headquarters at 41 Sacramento Street. The Citizens' Guard, sixty picked men led by Captain Olney, escorted the companies as they all marched off to the jail on Broadway to take Casey. A cannon was placed before the door. "I will go with them," said Casey, seeing no other way. Cora's presence was also requested. King died on May 19; Casey and Cora met their ends during his funeral, dangling from the second floor of the Vigilance Committee headquarters. "My faults are the result of my early education," said Casey. Two more bad fellows, Hetherington and Brace, were also hung. Then, on August 21, before disbanding, the Vigilance Committee held a parade on Third Street. By then there were four infantry regiments each with its own colors, two cavalry squadrons, battalions of artillery, riflemen, pistolmen, and police—over 6,000 men. Olney had become Brigadier General of all. The huge banner of the first Vigilance Committee was in a place of honor.

BATTALION CITIZENS GUARD

COMMITTEE OF VIGILANCE

THE VIGILANCE COMMITTEE

1851 and 1856

"It is an extremely serious thing for any organized community to throw over the orderly methods slowly and painfully developed through a thousand years of civilization, in the effort to rectify by violence the inefficacy or corruption of officials of its own choice, who can in our country always be changed with but little delay by safe and legal methods devised for the purposes."

—General Wistar

The 1851 Banner, on the wagon, presented by the Ladies of Trinity Church, was lost in 1906. It was made of blue satin with gilt lettering, shaded with darker blue and red. The banner of the Citizens Guard is shown minutely in a contemporary letter sheet. Black uniforms. See *Military Gazette*, August 30, 1856.

"Turning the American Constitution topsy-turvy."

IRISH CALIFORNIA

Irishmen came early to California. Timothy Murphy was here in 1828, settled at San Rafael in 1836 and hunted over the countryside with his hounds. Father Short came from Hawaii in 1832 and taught at Hartnell's school near Monterey. In 1845 Father McNamara asked the president of Mexico for a huge grant of land in California for an Irish colony of 10,000 souls. Otherwise, he said, "Your Excellency may be assured that before another year the Californias will form a part of the American union." And sure enough: the Stars and Stripes were soon flying everywhere. It was claimed later that a reason for the Bear Flag Revolt was to prevent McNamara from succeeding. The failures of the Irish potato crops of 1845-9 caused huge numbers of Irish folk to come to the United States in the '50s— 221,253 in 1851 alone. Many came to California and stayed. A beautifully painted flag led their procession to the mission in San Francisco on St. Patrick's Day, 1854.

THE PONY EXPRESS, next page

News was everything, and it had been coming to California from the East via Panama Steamer— a long, round-about way. Then in 1858, stages of Butterfield's Overland Mail came twice a week by way of 165 stations, on the wide sweep out of the way of the Southern Route, 19 days from Missouri to California, about the same time as the mail took on the steamers. Butterfield had a subsidy of $600,000 a year from the government, which was southern-controlled and opposed to any shorter, quicker northern route. William Russell's great Pony Express, the "Central Overland California and Pikes Peak Express Co.," was chartered without government money, and with fresh horses every 10-12 miles, begun on April 3, 1860, with William Richardson galloping westward. Each rider would change at least three horses and ride 75-100 miles; delivery was promised within 13 days from Missouri. A mochilla with four cantinas filled with mail was thrown over the saddle and quickly changed at each relay. The Express arrived at Placerville April 15. There, Bill Hamilton grabbed the mochilla from Warren Upson. He was delayed by a grand reception with bands and waving flags, but soon on he raced and reached Sacramento at 5:25 that day. There a celebration long remembered burst forth. Hamilton was met by Capt. Eyre's Sacramento Hussars, who rode furiously ahead of him from Sutter's Fort to J Street. From Sacramento the Pony Express went by the fast steamboat *Antelope* to San Francisco, where he arrived at 11:30 to shooting rockets and more cheers and the California Band playing "See the Conquering Hero Comes." The Fire Companies in their colorful uniforms escorted Hamilton and his gaily decorated pony, now wearing a woman's expensive bonnet, in a torch-lit parade to the *Alta Telegraph* office, the end of the trip. Soon, Sibley's Pacific and Overland Telegraph Companies—with government money—completed a wire to California on October 24, 1861. The last ride of the pony was near. Before long, the northern-controlled Congress would finance the Central Pacific Rail Road where the pony had ridden.

You know the color.
Annals of San Francisco, p. 524

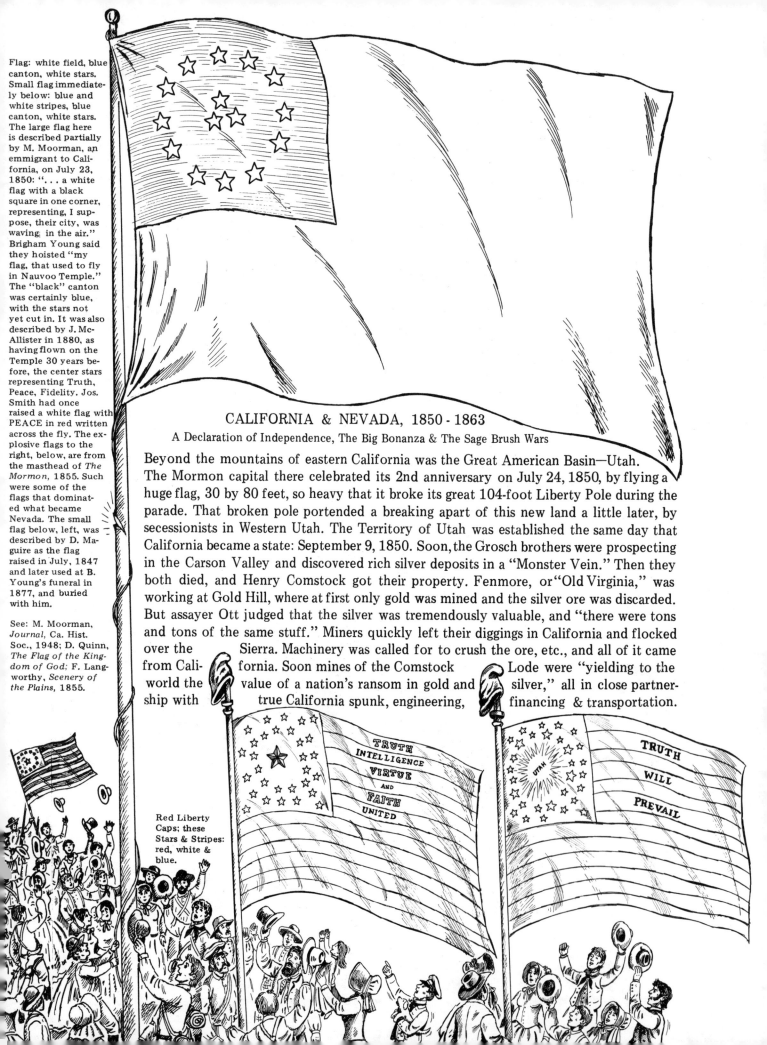

Flag: white field, blue canton, white stars. Small flag immediately below: blue and white stripes, blue canton, white stars. The large flag here is described partially by M. Moorman, an emmigrant to California, on July 23, 1850: "...a white flag with a black square in one corner, representing, I suppose, their city, was waving in the air." Brigham Young said they hoisted "my flag, that used to fly in Nauvoo Temple." The "black" canton was certainly blue, with the stars not yet cut in. It was also described by J. Mc-Allister in 1880, as having flown on the Temple 30 years before, the center stars representing Truth, Peace, Fidelity. Jos. Smith had once raised a white flag with PEACE in red written across the fly. The explosive flags to the right, below, are from the masthead of *The Mormon*, 1855. Such were some of the flags that dominated what became Nevada. The small flag below, left, was described by D. Maguire as the flag raised in July, 1847 and later used at B. Young's funeral in 1877, and buried with him.

See: M. Moorman, *Journal*, Ca. Hist. Soc., 1948; D. Quinn, *The Flag of the Kingdom of God*; F. Langworthy, *Scenery of the Plains*, 1855.

CALIFORNIA & NEVADA, 1850 - 1863
A Declaration of Independence, The Big Bonanza & The Sage Brush Wars

Beyond the mountains of eastern California was the Great American Basin—Utah. The Mormon capital there celebrated its 2nd anniversary on July 24, 1850, by flying a huge flag, 30 by 80 feet, so heavy that it broke its great 104-foot Liberty Pole during the parade. That broken pole portended a breaking apart of this new land a little later, by secessionists in Western Utah. The Territory of Utah was established the same day that California became a state: September 9, 1850. Soon, the Grosch brothers were prospecting in the Carson Valley and discovered rich silver deposits in a "Monster Vein." Then they both died, and Henry Comstock got their property. Fenmore, or "Old Virginia," was working at Gold Hill, where at first only gold was mined and the silver ore was discarded. But assayer Ott judged that the silver was tremendously valuable, and "there were tons and tons of the same stuff." Miners quickly left their diggings in California and flocked over the Sierra. Machinery was called for to crush the ore, etc., and all of it came from California. Soon mines of the Comstock Lode were "yielding to the world the value of a nation's ransom in gold and silver," all in close partnership with true California spunk, engineering, financing & transportation.

Red Liberty Caps; these Stars & Stripes: red, white & blue.

TRUTH INTELLIGENCE VIRTUE AND FAITH UNITED

TRUTH WILL PREVAIL

COLONEL CONNOR & THE 3rd CALIFORNIA INFANTRY Regt. march into Nevada & Utah, 1862

Soon thousands of new settlers were living in the Carson & other valleys; at a meeting at Gilbert's Saloon, a petition was drawn up for Congress: "We make known and declare our entire and unconditional separation from eastern Utah," said their Declaration of Independence. On March 2, 1861, the Territory of Nevada was established. But soon these seceders were quarreling with California, too. For one degree —60 miles of territory along a mutual boundary, was disputed. So in 1863 Sheriff Pierce of Plumas County, Cal., arrested Sheriff Naileigh of Roop County, N.T. A rescue was made and fighting began at Susanville. The Plumans, with an army of 100 or so, advanced on the Roopers; firing became general, parties were wounded and an armistice was made. Acting Governor Clemens of Nevada, Mark Twain's brother, soon settled all this with Governor Stanford of California. Aurora, another border town, was quarrelled over for two years by Mono County, Cal., and Esmeralda County, N.T., as it was the capital of both. Now these were Civil War times and in 1862 Aurora was thrown into pandemonium by a band of rebels. The most rabid rebel was arrested —and kicked Pvt. Steward on the shin, "which Mike responded to by a forcible presentation of his toe in the rebel's rear," while the town secessionists armed themselves. In the meantime, Colonel Connor of the Third Infantry, California Volunteers, took command of Utah and Nevada Territories. "Traitors shall not utter treasonable sentiments in this district with impunity," he said.

Blue regimental flag, gold fringe, stars, trim on scroll, letters; eagle: brown body, white head. Red, white and blue shield. Red scrolls. Blue and white tassels. Dark blue coats, sky blue trousers. Light blue trim on coats. Dark blue stripes on trousers. Red sash. Black hats with brass insignia. Gray blankets.

The Paiutes were peaceable until the Williams brothers waylaid their girls. Then they did bloody justice, whereupon Major Ormsby and 106 white avengers met the Indians at Pyramid Lake. There, young Chief Winnemucca outsoldiered Ormsby, who lost most of his men. Panic flew over the hills to California, and an army of a thousand hurried to the rescue.

Dark blue coats with light blue collars and cuffs; dark blue caps with light blue bands around bases; light blue pompon, epaulets on soldiers; gold epaulets on officer; light blue trousers with gold stripes. Brass buttons and belt plates. Brass eagle cap insignias.

THE PAIUTE WAR, 1860

THE
SIERRA GUARD
BATTALION
ORG. SEPT. 30, 1854
RE-ORG. MAR 24, 1856
DOWNIEVILLE

SIERRA GUARD BN
CALIFORNIA MILITIA

See
I. Murphy,
Life of Colonel Daniel Hungerford, 1891

From Downieville came Major Hungerford with his Sierra infantry battalion. Col. Jack Hays, mentioned before, was Commander-in-Chief of all. The big battle soon happened, and Major Hungerford, "...was able to save the day. Were it not for the discipline of his men, and his tactical manoeuvring . . . every man in the command would have been massacred. The well-conceived plan of young Winnemucca, the intelligent chief," was perceived. The Indians escaped to the Truckee River.

THE FIRST CALIFORNIA GUARD (Flying Artillery), "The Pioneer Corps of California," 1860

Colors: "The Company shall have two Silken colors and a silken guidon, the first on the National color of Stars and Stripes, the name of the Company to be embroidered with gold on the centre stripe. The second to be yellow, bearing in the centre two cannon crossing, with the letters, F.C.G. above, and the figure 1, below; fringe, yellow." Coat: dark blue, collar and cuffs of scarlet cloth, near the front a shell and flame of yellow metal; on each shoulder a scarlet worsted epaulette, secured by shoulder straps to be edged with gold braid; the front seams, seams of skirts and cuffs, to be edged with red cloth. Cap: dark blue cloth, band at the lower edge of the cap of scarlet cloth with an ornament in front of cross cannon of yellow metal; a red horse-hair plume to be worn with yellow metal spread eagle; the band to be edged with gold braid. Gilt buttons the same as for officers of artillery, USA with the letter A on the shield. Trousers: of white and light blue mixed cloth, commonly called "Army blue," with a stripe of scarlet cloth on each side, the stripe to be edged with gold braid. Chevrons of gold.

Bill of Dress, July 27, 1860

On July 27, 1849, in San Francisco at the school house on the plaza, 41 gentlemen organized an artillery corps (though they would also train with muskets) to be known as the "First California Guard." The army had been "inefficient," and the officers of the law needed help. Soon after this, many other guard units were formed, too. Here, the Guard are in the uniforms of 1860. "Although we have no State Military Academy, San Francisco possesses a military school—the Old Guard—the First California Guard . . . May she prove the West Point of California."* When the Civil War came, men of the Guard joined the California One Hundred, or California "Rangers," whom we will see presently. The Guard also provided soldiers for the Confederacy.

*S. F. Alta, Dec. 11, 1862

BEAR REPUBLIK

THE BEAR

BEARS

THE BEAR REPUBLIC

THE EL MONTE SECESSIONISTS
BRING BACK THE BEAR FLAG
May 4, 1861

If the Confederacy captures Washington, we will strike a blow here.

KNIGHTS OF THE GOLDEN CIRCLE

"California cherishes a loyal devotion to the union. Our honor and our pride are in its flag. . . California repudiates the suggestion of a Pacific republic."
—State Senator DeLong, 1861

El Monte was the home of old Texans, all determined secessionists. The Bear Flag, banner of break-away government, was painted and paraded there by about 200 of their Home Guard around patriotic Jonathon Tibbett's house. Many people had favored California with Oregon, etc. becoming a new country, the Pacific Republic, to weaken the north. Congressman Burch proposed a flag as shown. The El Monte boys were also Knights of the Golden Circle, a secessionist secret society.

PACIFIC REPUBLIC

*San Francisco Herald,
January 3, 1861
Ellison, California
and the Nation, 1927
Southern California,
Civil War Days, Hist.
Soc. So. Cal., 1921-4*

Dark blue coats, light blue trousers, stripes and trim; gold letters on Old Glory; blue regimental flag, brown American eagle, white head, yellow beak and talons, gold stars and arrowheads, green leaves, red and white stripes on shield, blue above, red scrolls, gold letters and edging

17,000 Californians volunteered for the Union army. Colonel Carleton commanded the 1st Regiment, which assembled in Oakland in 1861, camped near Los Angeles, then marched to San Diego and then to Fort Yuma. From there the "California Column" marched to retake New Mexico. The 2nd Regiment was at San Francisco, Santa Barbara and Fort Humboldt. The 3rd was at Stockton and under Colonel Connor went to Utah to protect the overland mail. The 4th, from Sacramento and the gold country, served in Oregon and Southern California. The 5th reinforced the California Column. The 6th was at Benicia and Humboldt; their flags, here, are preserved in the State Capitol. The 7th, from Sacramento and Marysville, went to Yuma, and the 8th, raised in San Francisco and San Jose, served in California.

"Edward D. Baker had saved the Pacific Coast to the Union."
—E. Kennedy

THE IMMORTAL COLONEL BAKER AND THE CALIFORNIA REGIMENT

(The Pennsylvania 71st Volunteer Regiment of Infantry)

And wheresoever that banner waves there glory may pursue and freedom be established.
—Col. Baker

Forward, my brigade, although someone has blundered.

See I. Wistar, *Autobiography*, 1937; Kennedy, *The Conquest for Cal. in 1861*, 1912; *Military Collector and Historian*, plate 495

Colonel Edward Baker, born in England, raised in Pennsylvania, had been a lawyer in Illinois, a congressman from there and a friend of Abe Lincoln. He led the 4th Regiment of Illinois Volunteers in the Mexican War, and won the Battle of Cerro Gordo when his commander was wounded. After the war he returned to Congress and on the death of President Taylor "delivered his celebrated eulogy on that great soldier, which immediately took rank as one of the most classic and elegant orations ever delivered in the American capitol." He came to California in '51 and soon became the

Colors: Zouave of the Baker Guards, blue jacket with red edging, brass buttons, blue vests, blue cap, light blue trousers, white leggings; guidon of the 72nd: blue silk, gold bumblebee on white oval Vivandiere of the 72nd: blue jacket, blue pants and tunic skirt, light gaiters, blue liberty cap with red band, green sash General Baker: regulation blue uniform

Colonel Baker, continued

most celebrated lawyer here. When Senator
Broderick was shot ("I die because I was
opposed to a corrupt administration and
the extension of slavery," he said) Baker
gave another immortal oration and immediately turned California right around for
the Union. Baker was invited to the new
state of Oregon in 1857 and became its
U.S. Senator. He returned to San Francisco
and gave the "greatest speech ever delivered
in California" for Lincoln, who carried the
state. When war began and Lincoln called
for volunteers, old Californians in New
York resolved to raise a regiment "to be
composed as far as possible of persons at
some time resident of California." Baker
was asked to be their colonel. It was raised
in Pennsylvania and mustered in New York,
Soon after, Baker led the Pennsylvania 69th
(Irishmen), 71st (his California Regiment),
72nd and 106th, until then also called the
California 1st, 2nd, 3rd and 5th regiments,
"Baker's Brigade," across the Potomac
River to the Battle of Ball's Bluff, Virginia.
Up an eighty-foot cliff the men went, into
the galling fire of the 8th Virginia Regiment. There was desperate hand-to-hand
fighting; the brave Baker fell at the head
of his men. Their colors, shot to tatters,
were lost* in the retreat across the river.
Of 570 men, 305 were lost in the action.
When news came over the new telegraph
line to California that the beloved Baker was dead, there was indescribable
grief, gloom and rage.

This page: "One patriotic citizen
named Mason. . . collected a gang
of cut-throats, unfurled to the
balmy breeze the three-barred
banner of the lost cause, declared for the Southern Confederacy, and robbed and
murdered all who failed
to pay him tribute. . .
The chief becoming en-
amored of the charms of
the wife of one of his band
was smiled on by the fair and
fickle one, which caused the reverse

White stars in the
blue canton;
red, white,
red stripes

of a smile in the
outraged husband,
who ended the
amorous dalliance
of the two guilty
lovers by putting
an end to the re-
doubtable Robin
Hood of the windy
pass."—*H. Bell*

*Later recovered and carried in the 4th of July parade in S.F., 1864

Southern California was overwhelmingly southern in sympathy in 1861, and 'Dixie' was the only tune heard anywhere ("dogs bark it, asses and mules bray it"). So the loyal Unionists of Los Angeles held a grand Union demonstration on May 25, a challenge to the secessionists. They received a warning beforehand that anyone raising the Stars and Stripes over the Court House would be shot dead; Unionists feared not. They met in the plaza; the army band played and the grand orator, Phineas Banning, an ardent abolitionist, gave a tumultuous speech and presented a large U.S. flag, the first raised in Los Angeles since the news of Fort Sumter.

THE CALIFORNIA HUNDRED, 1863

See: Orton, *Records of California Men in the War of the Rebellion*, 1890, p. 848; Uniforms: *Military Collector and Historian*, 1971; Flags: Capitol Museum, Sacramento

Mrs. Reed

A new recruit
is speaking now,
With laughing eyes
and sunny brow;
She whispers in
my listening ear,
"Come, take one
female volunteer. . .
'tis well, I'll keep thee
by my side,
With my brave hundred
thou shalt ride.
—Capt. J. S. Reed
according to J. Rogers

Uniforms: dark blue jackets and caps, light blue trousers, yellow stripes, chevrons, trim; Flag: dark blue, green wreath, red scrolls with gold edging and letters, State Seal: Minerva in gilt armor, brown bear, hills; blue sky

"A large number of young men in the State desired to go East and enter the army, and when it was found that the California Volunteers were being kept on this coast, a proposition was made to Massachusetts to raise a company here, and take it East." One hundred men under Captain Reed arrived at camp near Boston on January 4, 1863, and became Company A, 2nd Massachusetts Cavalry, and were ordered to the front in Virginia.

THE CALIFORNIA BATTALION

Flag text:
POTOMAC RIVER
ORANGE & ALEXANDRIA RR
SHENANDOAH VALLEY
JAMES RIVER
PETERSBURG

DEP'T OF WASHINGTON

SOUTH ANNA BRIDGE
BROOKVILLE
COYLES TAVERN
ASHBYS GAP
LITTLE RIVER PIKE
DRANESVILLE
RECTORTOWN
POINT OF ROCKS

ARMY OF THE POTOMAC

ALDIE
FREDERICK PIKE
TENALY TOWN
FORT RENO
FORT STEVENS
ROCKVILLE
POOLSV'
FORT STEVENS

SHERIDAN'S CAVA

SNICKERS GAP
NOLANS FORD
SHEPARDS TOWN
WHITE POST
MIDDLETOWN
KERNSTOWN
CEDAR
WINCHE

CALIFORNIA HUNDRED

ORGANIZED OCT 1862.
500 MUSTERED IN

CALIFORNIA CAVALRY BATT

BERRYVILLE PIKE
CHARLESTOWN
SUMMIT P
HALLTOWN
BERRY VILLE
SMITH FIELD
OPEQUAN CREEK
KNOX FORD
FRONT ROYAL
SNAKE MOUN
LURAT CT
MILLS FOR

GETTYSBURG CAMPAIGN, MOSBY'S GUERILLAS, E

MOUNT CRAWFORD
TOMS BROOK
STRASBURG
MADISON CT HOUSE
GORDONSVILLE
WHITE OAK ROAD
SOUTH ANNA
DINWIDDE CT HOUSE
FIVE FORKS
SOUTH

Four more companies were raised in California for the same regiment, sent to Washington and joined General Hooker's Army of the Potomac. They marched towards Gettysburg, then fought in many battles. At Hulltown, Captain Eigenbrodt, leading a charge, was killed, and the next day Lieutenant Meader fell, leading the Hundred. The battalion saw the meeting of Generals Grant and Lee at Appomattox and the surrender of the Army of Northern Virginia.

Orton, *Records of California Men*, 848-853
A. Hunt, *The Army of the Pacific*, 1951
Flag: Capitol Museum, Sacramento

The uniform is the same as opposite.

Flag: see the Calaveras *Californian*, May 6, 1948. "Despite the failure of Senator Jesse M. Mayo's resolution presented to the State Senate to replace the golden bear with the jumping frog, on the official state flag, it will be the frog —not the bear —who flies on the flag that will wave over Frog Town May 14, 15, 16, during the Calaveras Centennial Fair and Jumping Frog Jubilee . . ."

"California's bear has been chiefly employed in disturbing prospectors, sacking hen roosts, frightening women and children, while the frog has greatly enriched the world's literature." —Senator Jesse M. Mayo, 1948

*Watch for the gorgeous Bellerophon book, *Great Authors of California*.

LITERARY CALIFORNIA*
Mark Twain, 1865

CALIFORNIA REPUBLIC

One day Sam Clemens had to leave San Francisco in a hurry, and went to live up at Jackass Hill, and from there went to Angels Camp. There he got the story, wrote it up and sent it to Artemus Ward in New York; he gave it to the *Saturday Review*, where it appeared November 18, 1965. It is about Jim Smiley's frog Dan'l Webster: He "can outjump any frog in Calaveras County," said Smiley to a stranger, as $40 was bet that he could. Smiley went to find a frog for the stranger, while he, holding Smiley's frog, took out a teaspoon and "filled him pretty near up to his chin" with quail shot. Smiley soon returned from the swamp and handed the stranger his frog. " 'Now, if you're ready, set him alongside of Dan'l, . . . one-two-three-Git' . . . the new frog hopped off lively, but Dan'l gave a heave . . . but it warn't no use . . . The feller took the money and started away . . . 'I do wonder what in the nation that frog throw'd off for . . . he 'pears to look mighty baggy, somehow . . . Why bless my cats if he don't weigh five pounds.'—and turned him upside down and he belched out a double handfull of shot . . . he was the maddest man, . . . and took out after that feller, but he never ketched him." To celebrate, a jumping frog Jubilee began in 1928, and had its own flag in 1948.

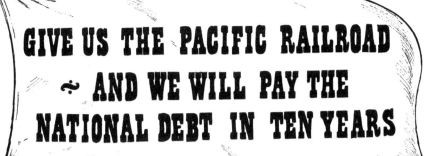

GIVE US THE PACIFIC RAILROAD ~ AND WE WILL PAY THE NATIONAL DEBT IN TEN YEARS

Ha! A flag celebrating Lincoln's reelection, flown March 4, 1865, Camp Douglas *Vedette* next day; cited in Fred Rogers, *Soldiers of the Overland*, 1938, p. 140.

"We have prayed and sighed for a railroad. . . If, four years ago, we had elected Frémont, in four months after, he would have recommended a railroad," speechified Col. Baker in 1859. "We are running a man now by the name of Lincoln (cheers) who will do the same thing. . . If he recommends a railroad—and he will—he won't twaddle about it." And he didn't. Engineer Judah determined that a railroad could be built over the Sierra Nevada mountains, and then persuaded these Sacramento shopkeepers of Lincoln's party to set up the company to do it. A road in the direction of the great

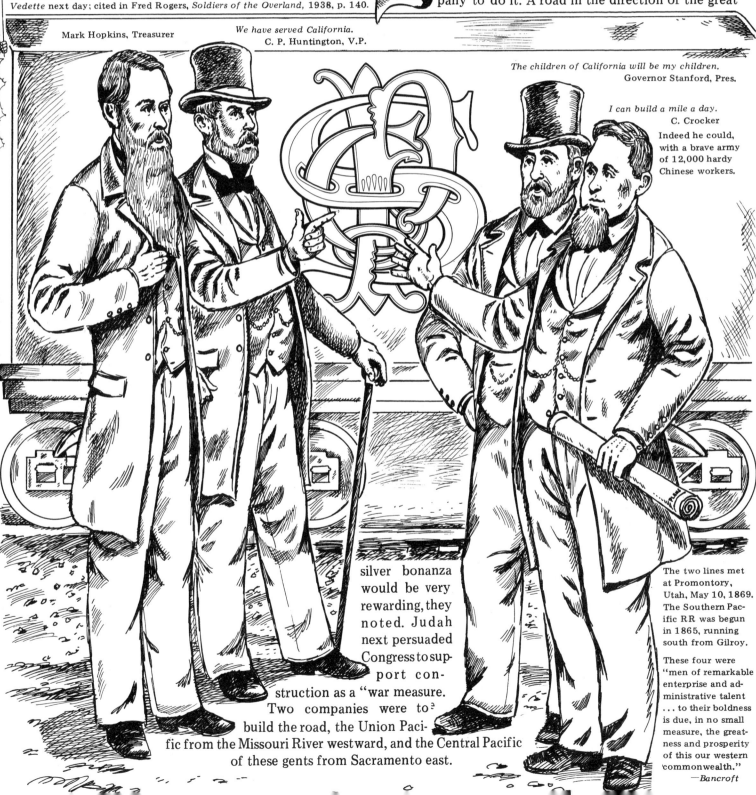

Mark Hopkins, Treasurer

We have served California.
C. P. Huntington, V.P.

The children of California will be my children.
Governor Stanford, Pres.

I can build a mile a day.
C. Crocker
Indeed he could, with a brave army of 12,000 hardy Chinese workers.

silver bonanza would be very rewarding, they noted. Judah next persuaded Congress to support construction as a "war measure. Two companies were to build the road, the Union Pacific from the Missouri River westward, and the Central Pacific of these gents from Sacramento east.

The two lines met at Promontory, Utah, May 10, 1869. The Southern Pacific RR was begun in 1865, running south from Gilroy.

These four were "men of remarkable enterprise and administrative talent . . . to their boldness is due, in no small measure, the greatness and prosperity of this our western commonwealth."
—*Bancroft*

Young Canby had come to California in 1849, a major with General Persifer Smith, commander of the department. Outrages against Indians were common then, and the government had been unable to stop them because soldiers kept running away to look for gold. Canby was here for two years; when he left he was full of strong feelings against the dastardly dealings towards the natives. After the Civil War, General Canby took command of the Army of the Columbia headquartered in Portland, Oregon. Settlers had been moving increasingly into Indian lands, and food became scarce. The Indians would have to steal or starve. The Modocs in Southern Oregon, who "never numbered over a thousand souls," under Keintpoos (Captain Jack), had left the Klamath reservation. Jack's father had been killed in the Ben Wright Massacre on Lost River in 1852, when Jack was 16. The Modocs felt they had been tricked into giving up their lands there, and they could not live with their enemies the Klamaths on the same reservation.

GENERAL CANBY, CAPTAIN JACK
AND THE MODOC WAR, 1873

I have been very solicitous that these Indians should be fairly treated, and have repeatedly used military force, lest they be wronged.

See:
J. Riddle, *Indian History of the Modoc War*, 1914

Guidon: blue canton, yellow stars and "B" and red and white stripes. Regimental flag: blue field, brown eagle with white head, yellow stars, red scrolls with yellow edges. Red, white and blue shield. Dark blue coats; light blue trousers; yellow chevrons; brass buttons and buckles. Black hats; blue caps. California "cannot grace her annals with a single Indian war bordering on respectability. It can boast, however, a hundred or two of as brutal butcherings on the part of the honest miners and brave pioneers, as any area of equal extent in our republic."—*Bancroft*, xxiv, 477.

Old Modoc Chief Schonchin had given up their ancient lands: "I think if we kill all white men, no more come. We kill and kill, but all time more come and more come . . . I fight no more," he had said. But in 1871 they wanted their old lands back, 14,000,000 acres. This made the settlers furious, for they also wanted the land. Then Captain Jack killed a Klamath enemy and was ordered arrested. The fierce Modocs became defiant, and determined to resist. There were just 71 Modoc warriors, and it was believed that Captain Jack's handsome sister, Queen Mary, incited them. Canby ordered the arrest of Captain Jack suspended and called it "impolitic if not cruel" to force the Modocs back to the reservation, which was without suitable resources. The settlers protested, and against Canby's wishes the Modocs were ordered back to the reservation. However, the Modocs refused even to discuss this, so on November 29, 1872, men of the 1st U.S. Cavalry surrounded the Modoc camp. Lt. Boutelle raised his pistol as warrior Charley shouldered his rifle, and both shot at once. The Modoc War was on. There were dead on both sides, and Modocs began killing settlers at Tule Lake where the Modocs had been at-

tacked. Canby sent all available troops to the scene, while the Modocs went to the lava beds in Northern California where Lt. Colonel Wheaton's troops attacked them on January 17, 1873. The battle raged all day. Wheaton lost 40 men and withdrew. The Modocs held their ground, a natural fortress. A peace commission was formed, but the Oregonians objected (ignoring "the future of the Indians," said Canby). The Modocs rejected everything anyway, for they didn't want to be shipped to Arizona. Canby met the chief on April 11 and said he was there to protect them. A few minutes later Captain Jack shot the general. Soon the starving Modocs surrendered. Captain Jack was hanged.

In 1874 the Woman's Crusade and the temperance movement boomed across the land. The Woman's Suffrage movement had been going for a few years, and many of the suffrage leaders were active in the temperance movement, too; there it was that they acquired battle skills. An important anti-liquor (local option) election was held in San Jose, and Sallie Hart, a fiery red-headed suffragette "with a tongue like a scorpion," bravely speechified against howling mobs of liquor men. A band of fifty small children paraded past the polls (where only men could vote), singing the famous songs and urging votes for cleaner living. The liquormen grew nasty; Sallie made speech after speech. The men got violent; Sallie was saved by the police. Though her cause that day was lost, the foe provided ample reason for future victory. A week later she rallied in Alameda; "The rum power," wrote the San Francisco *Post*, "looked with astonishment and then with alarm on the new crusade which the Local Option law inaugurated, and trembled at the new and potent force which came into the field, when women put their hands to the work." "One very unexpected result of the inroad of the Saloon Keepers Association upon Alameda is the creation of a sentiment favorable to female suffrage. We hear of persons who have always opposed it, who responded to Miss Sallie Hart's challenge."

SALLIE HART, SUFFRAGETTE
AND TEMPERANCE FIGHTER
SAN JOSE, JUNE, 1874

Local Option
WOMAN'S SUFFRAGE
1874 Crusade

TEMPERANCE

FATHER, DEAR FATHER COME HOME WITH ME NOW

Why should not I —American born, have as good a right to come here and exert an influence in behalf of what I believe to be just, as you?

SALOON KEEPERS ASSOC. FOREVER

San Jose *Mercury*, June 23, 26, 1874
San Francisco *Bulletin*, June 30, July 2, 1874; G. Ostrander, *The Prohibition Movement in California*, 1957

DENNIS KEARNEY & THE WORKINGMEN'S PARTY, 1877

After the gold mines declined in 1865 and the Central Pacific Railroad was completed in 1869, thousands of workers were found jobless. The Bank of California closed in 1875, and the stock market crashed. And there was hardly any rain in 1876/7; agriculture died. Eastern railroad strikes brought thousands of supporters to the sand lots in front of City Hall in San Francisco. A fiery Irish drayman, Dennis Kearney, became the chief agitator and founded the Workingmen's Party of California. He urged every workingman to buy a musket, and threatened to hang the capitalists. The party's object was "to wrest the government from the hands of the rich." Kearney appointed himself Brigadier General and organized military companies with uniforms and threatened guerilla warfare. But soon he fell out with other party leaders; his boisterous revolutionary talk made business stagnant! Good harvests soon returned and then prosperity.

Red flag, red beard on J. C. Day, vice-president; ship flags: Coleman's California Line, left, blue top and bottom, red sides, white center; Henry W. Peabody's Line, right, white flag, red letter

The reign of bloated knaves is over!

WORKINGMEN'S PARTY OF CALIFORNIA

Thieves, peculators, land-grabbers, bloated bond-holders, rail-road magnates and shoddy aristrocrats.

The cry against capital was then thought unwise, for without it there could be no development-or jobs. After a short, wild existence, the Workingmen's Party disappeared. Kearney became a real estate broker and soon was a capitalist himself. Viva California!

ITALIAN CALIFORNIA: A. P. GIANNINI, ENRICO CARUSO & THE EARTHQUAKE, APRIL 18, 1906

San Francisco in 1906 had California's largest Italian settlement—North Beach, a rather successful place. A.P. Giannini would soon make it, and the whole state of California, more prosperous still. On August 10, 1904, near the jail, he opened the Bank of Italy, "to serve the little fellow." Twenty months later, San Francisco shook apart, and A.P.'s bank promptly helped put it back together again. The other greatest Italian since Augustus or the Medici, Caruso, just happened to be in San Francisco on April 18, 1906, where he was about to sing in a benefit for the victims of a recent eruption of Mt. Vesuvius. But the San Andreas fault's bouncing near San Francisco, destroying the opera house and 28,000 other buildings, also shook the great tenor. " 'Ell of a place," he said; "I never come back here."

We are going to rebuild San Francisco and it will be better than ever.

BANCA D'ITALIA
BANK OF ITALY

BANK OF ITALY
BANCA D'ITALIA
$

BANK OF ITALY
$

RUMBLE RUMBLE

RUMBLE

GIVE ME VESUVIU...

Teddy Roosevelt
TR

Flags of the Kingdom of Italy: green, white, red tricolor; red shield with the white cross of Savoy, surrounded by a blue border. The bank's customers complained if the Italian tricolor wasn't flown when they thought it should be. *Cal. Hist. Soc. Quarterly*, September, 1968

Note: A.P.'s father was from a village near Genoa and settled in San Jose where A.P. was born in 1870. Caruso escaped the earthquake with a prized autographed photograph of President Roosevelt. He had felt his bed rocking like a boat at 5:00 A.M. He looked out the window, saw buildings toppling, and was soon seen wandering downtown in his pajamas and fur coat.

CALIFORNIA PICTURE COMPANY

GO BEARS

GO CAL

CAL FOREVER!

UNIVE of CALI

WE LOV CALI

CAL

UC

CALIF.

CALIFORNIA

CAL

UC

BEARS

CAL

UC FOREVER

UC

UC

UC FOREVER

UC FOREVER

The movie business was once California's greatest glory. In the sunshine of Southern California—perfect for shooting outdoors scenes—a Scots gent, Robert Brunton, in about 1913 found an empty barn for a studio on Sunset Boulevard, surrounded by oak or "holly" trees. And there he put Mack Sennett to work. Soon, Jesse Lasky and his sister Blanche hired young Cecil B. DeMille to film in the neighborhood, and Hollywood had become movie land. Then the hilarious Harold Lloyd arrived; he is shown here with the masthead flag of *The Freshman*, filmed during an actual game up in the Berkeley stadium in 1924. How much joy Hollywood has given the world is incalculable. And how much cash flow it has given California is also, I suppose.

Flag colors: Blue and Gold, of course, even though the movie was black and white.

WINKIE - MUNCHKIN
GILLIKIN - QUADLING

"How lucky we were to discover this beautiful country," exclaimed Trot in *The Scarecrow of Oz*, (1915, Ch. 9). "The country seems rather high class, I'll admit, Trot," said Cap'n Bill. "No one could live in such a country without being happy and good," added Trot, who was a true California girl. And California is where Mr. Baum had moved when he wrote these words and ten of the fourteen wonderful books of Oz.* He had written successful plays, done Shakespeare, raised chickens, dealt in oil, gone broke, become a Dakota merchant, gone broke, moved to Chicago, written for a newspaper, turned travelling salesman (crockery), started a magazine, and rooted for the Cubs.

He'd surely end up in California. And all along he told lots of children lots of truly delightful stories. "Write them down," said his mother-in-law, and he did; in 1900 *The Wonderful Wizard of Oz* appeared and was a sudden best seller.

* He took the name from from his file cabinet, O - Z.

Flag: "They played the National air called 'The Oz Spangled Banner,' and behind them were the standard bearers with the Royal flag. This flag was divided into four quarters, one being colored sky-blue, another pink, a third lavender and a fourth white. In the center was a large emerald-green star, and all over the four quarters were sewn spangles that glittered beautifully in the sunshine. The colors represented the four countries of Oz, and the green star the Emerald City."
—*Dorothy and the Wizard in Oz*, (1908, Ch. 1

The next two Oz books were written in Michigan; the fourth, *Dorothy and the Wizard in Oz*, was written in Coronado, California, where the Baums wintered in 1907/8. This book had a California setting, with an earthquake like San Francisco's of 1906. Mr. Baum wrote nine more Oz books in California, as well as dozens of others. But his first love was the stage; the first Oz books had been made into a wonderful operetta, and made Mr. Baum rich. Other ventures failed, and broke him. His stories were handy for the new medium—the movies. Baum hired Selig and his Polyscope machine in 1908 to make a movie of *The Land of Oz*. Mr. Baum narrated while an orchestra made music; his eldest son was the projectionist. This lost money, too. The Baums, though, like all of us, preferred California to anywhere else, anyway. So here they came for good. They moved to 149 N. Magnolia Avenue in Los Angeles—"never had any city in any fairyland ever equalled this one in stately splendor," he wrote (*Scarecrow in Oz*, Ch. 21). Soon after they bought a lot at 1749 Cherokee Avenue, Hollywood, and there they built Ozcot. Mr. Baum then noticed the new industry growing up in his neighborhood and formed the Oz Film Manufacturing Company with a studio on Santa Monica Boulevard. The first picture was *The Patchwork Girl of Oz*, five reels, and it failed too. "In life, nothing adverse lasts very long," he later wrote. After 1915 Mr. Baum stuck to writing Oz books, playing golf in Griffith's Park, raising Rhode Island reds, playing with Toto, his cocker spaniel, growing prize chrysanthemums, looking after his hundreds of beautiful birds, and corresponding with children. He died in 1919, midway between the California Gold Rush and today. In no make-believe land have such wonders ever happened as in these eras. He is buried in Forest Lawn in Glendale. In 1925 Oliver Hardy played *The Tin Woodman* in a film, and in 1939, MGM made their great masterpiece. Oz surely lives forever, and the closest thing to it is our California.

"Things had to be dreamed of before they became realities," said Mr. Baum. "So I believe that dreams . . . are likely to lead to the betterment of the world. The imaginative child will become the imaginative man or woman most apt to create, invent, and therefore to foster civilization." *The Lost Princess of Oz*, Preface

THE WOBBLIES & THE WHEATLAND RIOT
August 3, 1913, near Marysville

Red flag, yellow letters

I.W.W.

IT'S FOR THE KIDS!

I.W.W.

DURST HOPS WHEATLAND

See H. Weintraub,
The I.W.W. in Cal.,
UCLA, 1947

Nearly half of all large-scale farms in the U.S. were then (and are now) in Cal. They did their harvesting with poor, migrating labor, often calling in many more hands than needed to keep wages unmercifully low. The Wobblies—I.W.W., Industrial Workers of the World, founded in 1905, were always on the move. On a hot August 3, 1913, 2,800 men, women and children camped near Durst's hop ranch at Wheatland, near Marysville. There were few toilets—and no water. The stench was terrible, and there was dysentery. Little children, 5-10 years old, worked in the fields in the 105°heat. The Wobblies were there to organize the unhappy people. Blackie Ford was holding a sick baby, leading a Wobbly song, when the sheriff and his men arrived with Durst's lawyer, the District Attorney. A deputy fired a shot, and fighting began. The District Attorney, a deputy and two workers were killed. The posse fled. The governor called the National Guard up to Wheatland. Wobblies were arrested there and throughout California. Blackie and Herman Suhr, who had been through Wobbly battles in Fresno and San Diego, were arrested and sentenced to life in prison. But from this Californians learned how bad the conditions of migratory workers were.

A new local (38-79) of the International Longshoremen's Assn. began in San Francisco in 1933. Dock workers had many objections to existing conditions, so almost everyone joined. Their demands were made; the employers objected; a strike began, and a thousand men marched peacefully in a picket line. Soon the Teamsters joined; Sailors, Boilermakers, Machinists, Ferryboatmen, Warehousemen followed. The angry ship owners vowed to "open the port." The police opened fire at Pier 18, and the Embarcadero became a battlefield. Chief Quinn's mounted men fired gas bombs and shotguns; the strikers' weapons were Old Glory and the I.L.A. banner; guess who would win?

BLOODY THURSDAY
The Great Maritime Strike
San Francisco, July 5, 1934

On July 3, at Pier 38, Capt. Hoertkorn waved his gun and actual war raged. Fallen men and blood puddles were everywhere. Governor Merriam called out the National Guard, which marched in with machine guns and bayonets. It was "Bloody Thursday," July 5, 1934, and Howard Sperry and Nick Bordoise lay dead. 40,000 people marched up Market Street at their funeral and a General Strike closed down the sorrowful city. California truly owes these martyrs a debt.

Flag: blue field, gold letters; see M. Quinn, *The Big Strike*, 1949. For years Bellerophon Books had their offices on Steuart Street and the Embarcadero, next to where the I.L.A. hall had been. Every anniversary of Bloody Thursday we passed by with great respect as the old men of the union held a quiet ceremony there. "We are here to pay the respects of labor to you, Howard Sperry, and you, Nicholas Bordoise," they'd say.

CALIFORNIA AND JAPAN: SUBMARINE I-17 ATTACKS ELLWOOD, FEBRUARY 23, 1942, 7:07 P.M.

In California, we owe the Japanese for much more than just their exquisitely made products today. In 1882, due to outrageous racial prejudices, the Chinese were excluded from California; there were 132,200 Chinese here then, and only 86 Japanese. The sugar beet industry soon sorely missed the Chinese, so in 1890 Japanese were "invited" here to do the work. They were considered "very valuable immigrants" as skilled seasonal workers. By 1900, 24,326 Japanese had come to California, and by 1909 they were 43% of the state's farm labor supply. Soon they were dominant in intensive agriculture, cultivating celery, berries, asparagus, cantaloupe, and garden crops generally. Japanese who came to California were efficient, experienced farmers, and very industrious; "they created new crop industries, and expanded the demand for farm labor. Because of their skill and industry, the Japanese brought about great changes in California agriculture. It is impossible to appraise adequately the full extent of their remarkable contributions." Their timing and planning of year-round production was carefully worked out, and Californians' diets were considerably improved. They developed successful orchards, vineyards, and gardens on land of little or no value before. So successful were they, though, that jealousy soon brought on anti-Japanese sentiment. They were model citizens but their "hunger to own land, and ability to achieve it," brought on an hysterical campaign against them. This resulted in an undeclared "California-Japanese War" (1900-1942),* with the exclusion of Japanese from San Francisco's schools, 1906; the Alien Land Act, 1913—aimed at driving the Japanese out of California; another such act in 1920, which nearly brought us to war with Japan; and an exclusionary Immigration Act, 1924. Each of these brought fierce resentment in Japan. Four days before this scene, the infamous Executive Order No. 9066 was signed; it had been needlessly called for by General De Witt, Western Defense Command, at the behest of politicians like Earl Warren and publishers McClatchy and Hearst. Without charges, hearings or due process, 112,533 people of Japanese ancestry, 80% from California, 70,000 of them U.S. citizens, were put in concentration camps. In spite of this, 33,000 young Japanese Americans joined our armed forces. Many went into the 100th Infantry Battalion and the 442nd Regimental Combat Team, and their immortal deeds absolutely shine in our history.

* C. McWilliams, *Factories in the Field*, 1939, and *Prejudice*, 1944

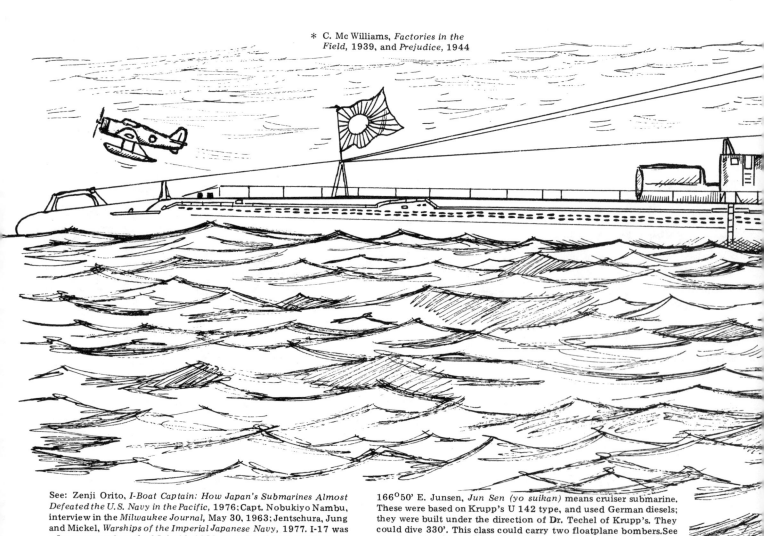

See: Zenji Orito, *I-Boat Captain: How Japan's Submarines Almost Defeated the U.S. Navy in the Pacific*, 1976; Capt. Nobukiyo Nambu, interview in the *Milwaukee Journal*, May 30, 1963; Jentschura, Jung and Mickel, *Warships of the Imperial Japanese Navy*, 1977. I-17 was a Junsen type, launched July 19, 1939, completed January 24, 1941 and sunk November 25, 1943 40 miles S.E. of Noumea, 23°26' S.,

166°50' E. Junsen, *Jun Sen (yo suikan)* means cruiser submarine. These were based on Krupp's U 142 type, and used German diesels; they were built under the direction of Dr. Techel of Krupp's. They could dive 330'. This class could carry two floatplane bombers. See also: Naval Inst. Press, *Submarines of the Imp. Japanese Navy*, 1986.

Two months, two weeks and two days after Pearl Harbor, just at dusk, as President Roosevelt began a fireside radio chat to the nation, Captain Kizo Nishino ordered "Battle surface" to the seventy-man crew of His Imperial Japanese Majesty's submarine I-17. They were right off the Ellwood oilfield, near where today lies the campus of the University of California at Santa Barbara. Captain Nishino took the bridge, and five crewmen and a gunnery officer rushed on deck and began firing their only gun, a 5", 40 caliber weapon. They had been off San Diego and were unable to find a ship within range. But there they had received a radio message from the Commander of the Submarine Fleet to attack either a highway or a factory, to distract American warships. They went quietly north, and then, "We are the first to attack America! " said a crewman. And indeed they were, the first since the War of 1812. "Even if we didn't hit a thing, they know I-17 has been here. All of us felt like heroes," said sailor Nagera. "What did we hit? " Gunner Onodes said he didn't know. "I only saw flashes," he said. Lt. Nambu, in charge of torpedoes, from below heard cars on Highway 101 braking as the firing started, and air raid sirens followed. He rushed up the hatch to have a look. Red lights were flashing, racing to the scene. It took three minutes to fire twenty shells, and then I-17 submerged and left. Airplanes were coming, so a fake bamboo periscope was left floating to fool them. The searching planes dropped flares, but by then the I-17 was far away. Next she sank a ship thirty-five miles below San Francisco with two torpedoes, and then another off Cape Mendocino with one torpedo. From shore came reports of a worried America. The submarine was "so big I thought it might have been a cruiser or a destroyer," reported oil worker Brown. "Some of the shells landed awfully close," he added. "BOLD RAID," raged the local paper; "with diabolical cunning and boldness the enemy craft struck . . . shot after shot whined and whistled over the oil field . . . the explosions were shattering in their force. Buildings rocked as during an earthquake. Geysers of earth shot heavenward."* "Just like in the movies," said Mrs. Wheeler, who ran the nearby cafe. "There was a kind of indignation and surprise that anyone would dare to do this to us—would dare to shell the United States," she added on the radio.

!?!

Flag: red Rising Sun;
red and white rays

* LA Examiner, LA Times,
SB News Press, Feb. 24, 25, 1942

THE UNITED STATES MARINES TAKE OVER RANCHO SANTA MARGARITA Y LAS FLORES, 1942

In August, 1942, the Ninth U.S. Marine Regiment was ordered to march up from San Diego to establish their new Camp Pendleton, formerly the great Rancho Santa Margarita y Las Flores, 141,000 acres near Oceanside. On September 1, Lt. Col. Lemuel Shepherd (later Commandant of the Corps) and the Ninth set out; they arrived four days later, having fought simu- lated attacks all the way. Not long afterwards, Marines from Camp Pendleton fought the great Pacific battles of World War II. Many did not return.

NINTH MARINES F.M.F.

SEMPER FIDELIS

Command Battle Standard (Type III, Class 1): red field and letters; gold emblem with silver seas; gold scrolls, fringe and tassels; Marine green uniforms; khaki webbing.

Light blue flag of the UNO

"This occasion shows again the continuity of history. By this Charter, you have given reality to the ideal of that great statesman of generation ago. . .Woodrow Wilson."

CBS   NBC   CBS

"The Charter of the United Nations . . . is a solid structure upon which we can build a better world . . . it is a declaration of great faith by the nations of the earth—faith that war is not inevitable, faith that peace can be maintained . . . What you have accomplished in San Francisco shows how well the lessons of military and economic cooperation have been learned. You have created a great instrument for peace and security and human progress in the world . . . Artificial and uneconomic trade barriers should be removed—to the end that the standard of living of as many people as possible throughout the world may be raised. . ."

—Harry S Truman

RESIDENT HARRY S TRUMAN & THE FORMING OF THE UNITED NATIONS, SAN FRANCISCO, June 26, 1945

CALIFORNIA & SPACE: SHUTTLE LANDINGS AT EDWARDS AIR FORCE BASE

NATIONAL AERONAUTICS AND SPACE ADMINISTRATION
U.S.A.
Columbia
NASA
United States
USA
México

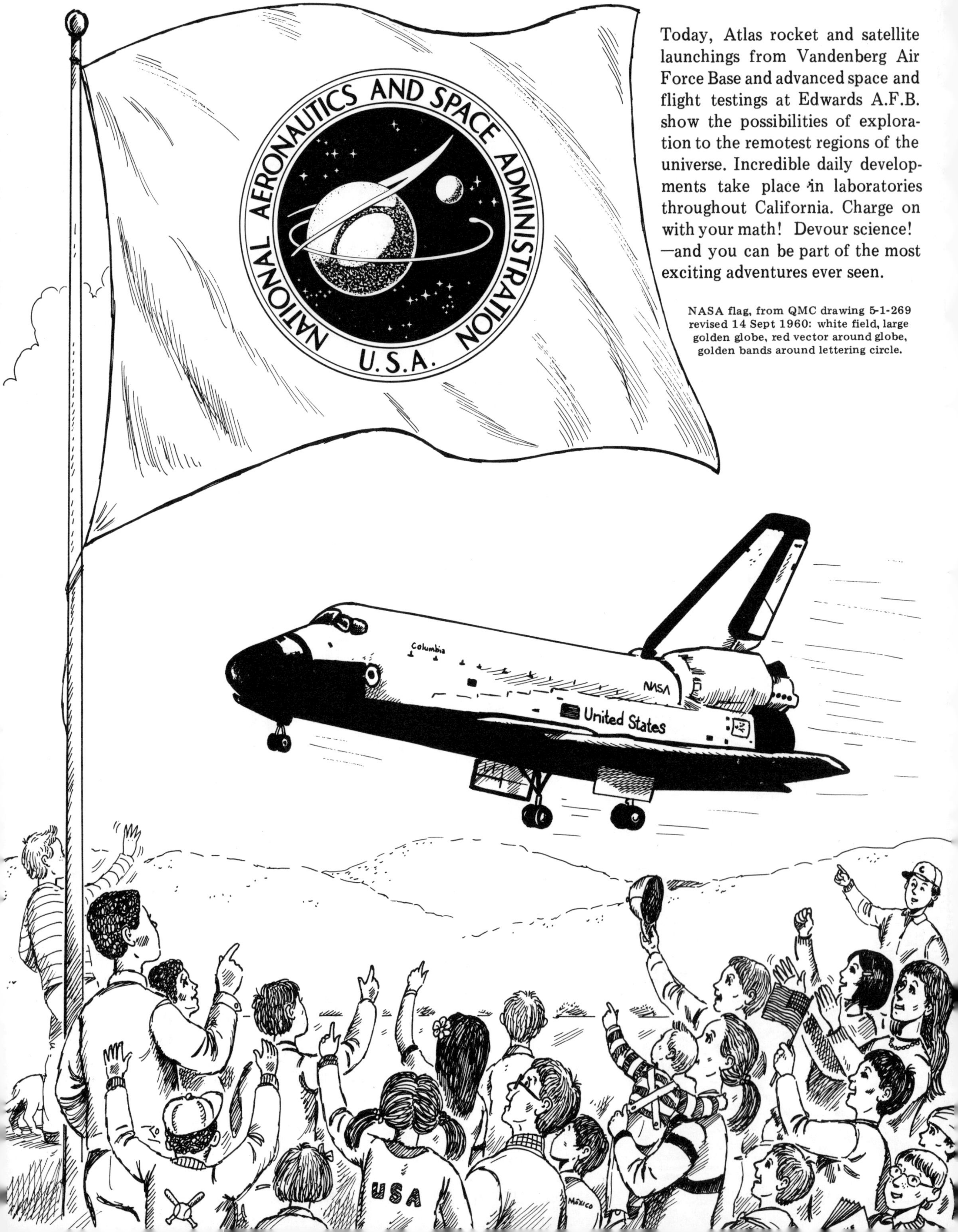

Today, Atlas rocket and satellite launchings from Vandenberg Air Force Base and advanced space and flight testings at Edwards A.F.B. show the possibilities of exploration to the remotest regions of the universe. Incredible daily developments take place in laboratories throughout California. Charge on with your math! Devour science! —and you can be part of the most exciting adventures ever seen.

NASA flag, from QMC drawing 5-1-269 revised 14 Sept 1960: white field, large golden globe, red vector around globe, golden bands around lettering circle.